killer whale karl

horace sea horse

starfish stuckey

octo eddy

meanie marlin

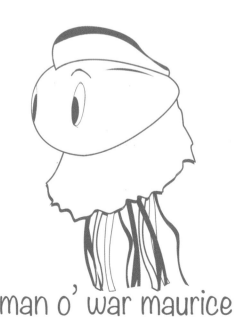

man o' war maurice

For Natalie and Gisele
with love, Lance

This is a work of fiction. Any names are used fictitiously
or are the product of the author's imagination.
Sharky Marky was printed by:
WORZALLA
3535 Jefferson Street • Stevens Point, Wisconsin 54481
March 2015:

Summary: A shark participates in an undersea racing adventure.
IBSN: 0-9895712-2-7 (hardcover: akl.paper) [1. Shark -- Fiction.
2. Marine Life -- Fiction. 3. Racing -- Fiction.

Sharky Marky

And the Scavenger Hunt

Lance Olsen

Thomas Perry

The undersea racetrack is busy today.
The racers are waiting to be underway.
Starfish Stuckey polishes up Marky's car;
So it can go—**Fast, Quick,** and **Far...**

Today there's a race of an unusual kind.
The drivers have a list of things they must find.
Winning is not just about being out in front.
They must find all the items;
It's a **Scavenger Hunt!**

Sharky Marky is ready for the race to begin.
He'll try his best—he sure wants to win!

Red Light!

The racers are ready. They're all on their marks.

Yellow Light!!

Get set! It's almost time to start.

Green Light!!!

Go, Marky, Go!!!

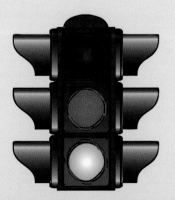

Algae

Marky scoops up some *Algae*, his first on the list.
As he speeds by Eddy—it creates quite a mist.

Marky grabs a **Barnacle**—it's holding on tight.
Bartholomew sees him pulling with all of his might.

Barnacle

Clam

Man O' War Maurice speeds off with a **Clam**.
Grab one, Marky—before those clams scram!

Sally Sea Lion finds a few colored **Dice**.
She throws one to Marky—now isn't that nice!

Dice

Earmuffs

Some fuzzy **_Earmuffs_** rest on an old broken dock.
Marky grabs a pair—he's sure on the clock!

A number of **Frisbees** are stuck in the sand.
Marky speeds off with one in his hand.

Frisbee

Guitar

Peter Puffer drives by a yellow **Guitar**.
Marky takes it and plays it—he could be a star!

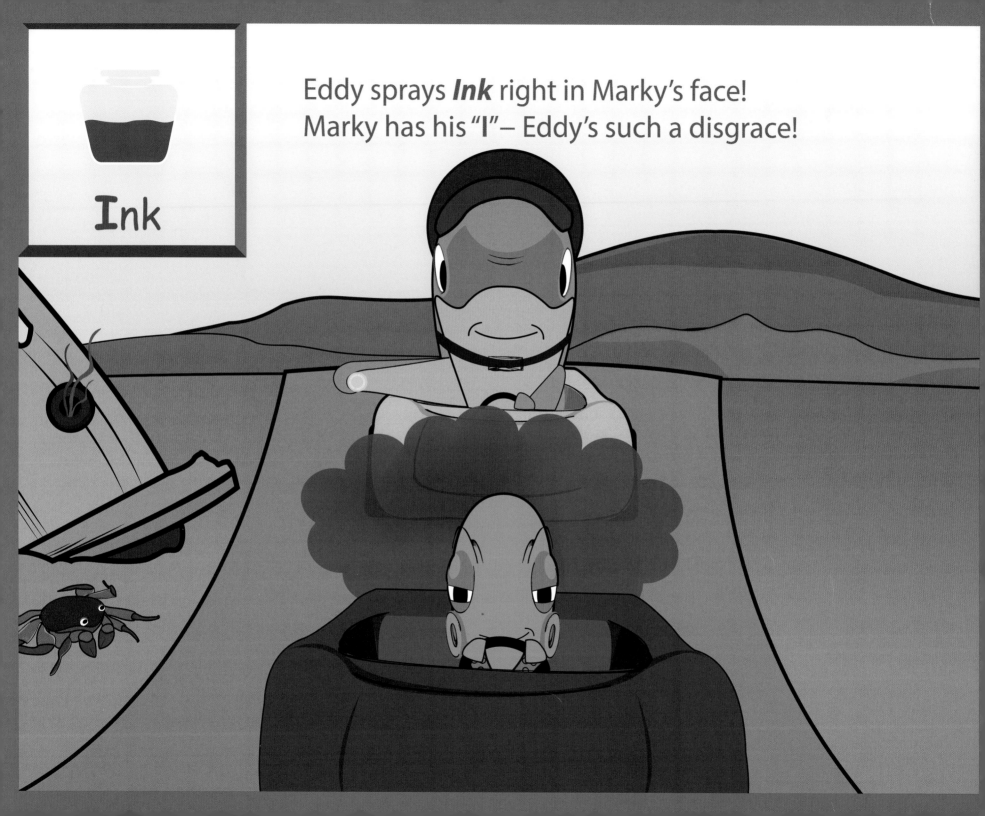

Marky stops to grab a dirty old *Jug*.
It sat on top of a handwoven rug.

Jug

Kite

Diego Dolphin is tangled up in a *Kite.*
Marky stops racing to make sure he's alright!

Meanie Marlin poked a **Lantern** in the sand.
Meanie only took one—isn't that grand?

Lantern

Mirror

Maurice grabs two **Mirrors** by a broken down truck.
He offers one to Marky—oh, what luck!

Marky grabs a **Necklace** and puts it on Sally. That's a nice gesture that adds to her tally.

Necklace

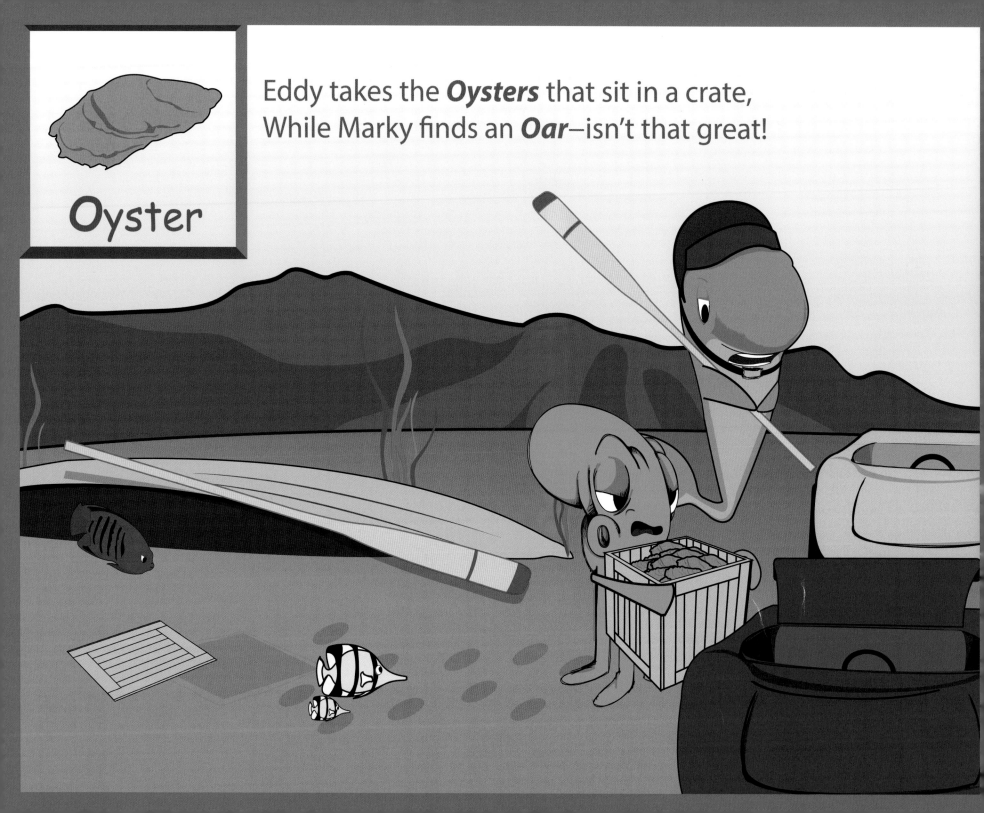

Oyster

Eddy takes the **Oysters** that sit in a crate,
While Marky finds an **Oar**—isn't that great!

Quill

Marky finds some **Quills** that sat on a chair.
He hands one to Bartholomew; it's important to share!

Two lobsters play tennis next to a car.
Marky snags a **Racket** that sat in a jar.

Racket

Shoe

A saltwater croc guards a smelly old **Shoe.**
Be careful, Marky—just drive on through!

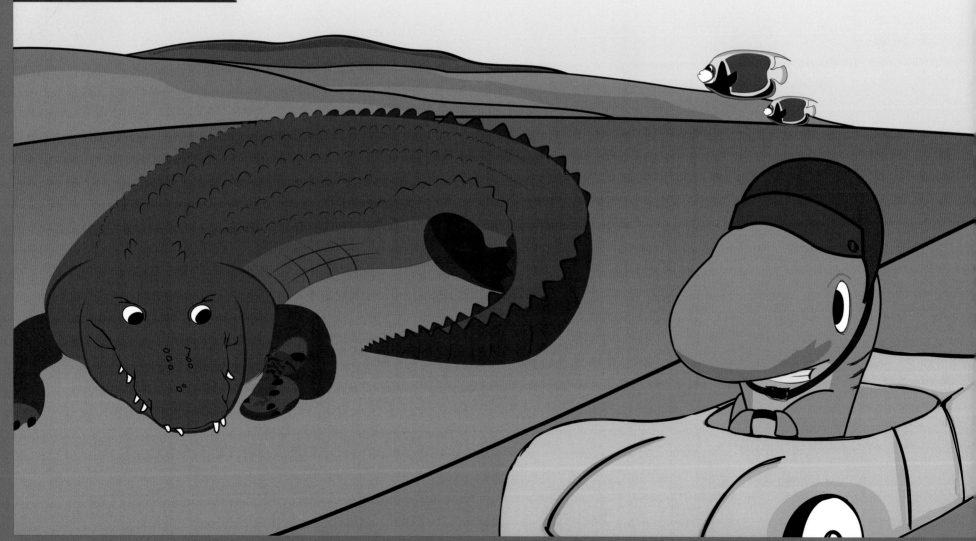

Urchin

Spiny **Urchins** live on an old sunken ship.
Marky picks one up—careful with your grip!

The racers spot **Vases** in a wide-open space.
They better grab one fast to earn first place!

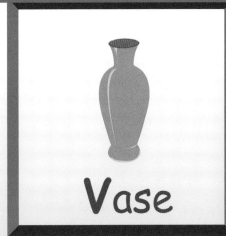

Vase

Whistle

A family of ducks cross the undersea track.
Horace blows a **Whistle** to bring a stop to the pack!

Walrus Whippleton plays a **_Xylophone_** with glee.
Marky cringes and squirms—he's singing off key!

Xylophone

Yo-Yo

Marky spots a **Yo-Yo** twisted in a reef.
It's not that stuck—oh, what a relief!

As the race ends we find Eddy in front...
Now we must find out who won the hunt!

The racers match their treasures to what's on the list.
Let's find out what everyone missed!

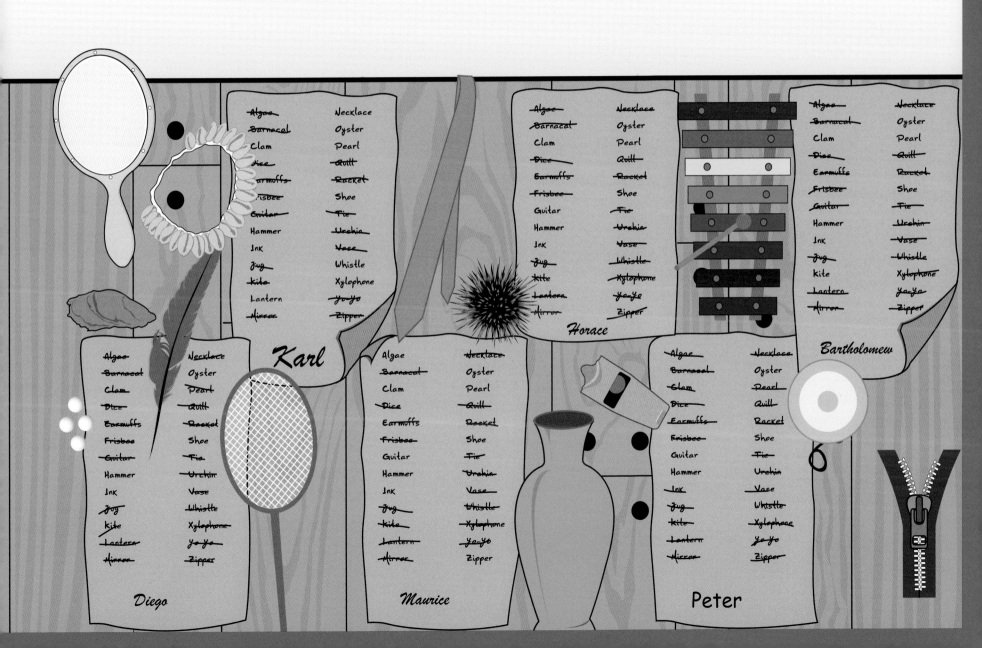

Karl

~~Algae~~   Necklace
~~Barnacal~~ Oyster
Clam   Pearl
~~Dice~~   ~~Quill~~
~~Earmuffs~~ ~~Racket~~
~~Frisbee~~ Shoe
~~Guitar~~   ~~Tie~~
Hammer   ~~Urchin~~
Ink   ~~Vase~~
~~Jug~~   Whistle
~~Kite~~   Xylophone
Lantern   ~~Yo-yo~~
~~Mirror~~   ~~Zipper~~

Horace

~~Algae~~   Necklace
~~Barnacal~~ Oyster
Clam   Pearl
~~Dice~~   ~~Quill~~
Earmuffs   ~~Racket~~
~~Frisbee~~ Shoe
Guitar   ~~Tie~~
Hammer   ~~Urchin~~
Ink   ~~Vase~~
~~Jug~~   ~~Whistle~~
~~Kite~~   ~~Xylophone~~
~~Lantern~~ ~~Yo-yo~~
~~Mirror~~   ~~Zipper~~

Bartholomew

~~Algae~~   ~~Necklace~~
~~Barnacal~~ Oyster
Clam   Pearl
~~Dice~~   ~~Quill~~
Earmuffs   ~~Racket~~
~~Frisbee~~ Shoe
~~Guitar~~   ~~Tie~~
Hammer   ~~Urchin~~
Ink   ~~Vase~~
~~Jug~~   ~~Whistle~~
Kite   Xylophone
~~Lantern~~ ~~Yo-yo~~
~~Mirror~~   ~~Zipper~~

Diego

~~Algae~~   Necklace
~~Barnacal~~ Oyster
~~Clam~~   ~~Pearl~~
~~Dice~~   ~~Quill~~
~~Earmuffs~~ ~~Racket~~
~~Frisbee~~ Shoe
~~Guitar~~   ~~Tie~~
Hammer   ~~Urchin~~
Ink   Vase
~~Jug~~   ~~Whistle~~
Kite   ~~Xylophone~~
~~Lantern~~ ~~Yo-yo~~
~~Mirror~~   ~~Zipper~~

Maurice

Algae   ~~Necklace~~
~~Barnacal~~ Oyster
Clam   Pearl
~~Dice~~   ~~Quill~~
Earmuffs   ~~Racket~~
~~Frisbee~~ Shoe
Guitar   ~~Tie~~
Hammer   ~~Urchin~~
Ink   ~~Vase~~
~~Jug~~   ~~Whistle~~
~~Kite~~   ~~Xylophone~~
~~Lantern~~ ~~Yo-yo~~
~~Mirror~~   Zipper

Peter

~~Algae~~   Necklace
~~Barnacal~~ Oyster
~~Clam~~   ~~Pearl~~
~~Dice~~   Quill
~~Earmuffs~~ ~~Racket~~
~~Frisbee~~ Shoe
Guitar   ~~Tie~~
Hammer   Urchin
~~Ink~~   ~~Vase~~
~~Jug~~   Whistle
~~Kite~~   ~~Xylophone~~
~~Lantern~~ ~~Yo-yo~~
~~Mirror~~   ~~Zipper~~

Did Eddie win? He had the most treasure...
No! A cheater can't win by anyone's measure.

Who won the **Scavenger Hunt**, can <u>YOU</u> take a guess?
Sharky Marky of course, he found more than the rest!

Fun Definitions

Algae: Little Tiny plants that float in the ocean.

Barnacle: A tiny crustacean that sticks to objects under the water and forms a shell to protect itself.

Clam: A shellfish with two light colored shells .

Dice: Small cubes with dots on the sides.

Earmuffs: Mittens to cover your ears when it's cold.

Frisbees: A plastic disk you can toss to a friend.

Guitar: A musical instrument with six strings and a long neck.

Hammer: A tool with a metal head used to hit nails into wood.

Ink: Colored liquid used for writing or printing.

Jug: A large container to hold liquid.

Kite: A fun toy you can fly on a string.

Lantern: A light that has a bulb or flame that can be carried by hand from the top.

Mirror: a piece of glass that is not see through but reflects the image facing it.

Necklace: Jewelry worn around your neck.

Oysters: A shellfish with two dark and rough shells.

Pearls: A tiny white and shiny ball found inside an oyster.

Quills: A feather from a bird that can be used for writing.

Racket: A stick with a large oval on the end used to hit a ball or other object.

Shoe: A special covering for your whole foot with a stiff bottom to protect your foot from things on the ground.

Tie: A ribbon wrapped around a persons neck that is passed over and though itself to form a knot or bow.

Urchin: A small sea animal covered in sharp pointy spines.

Vase: A container used for holding flowers.

Whistle: A shaped piece that when blown into, creates a varied vibration or noise.

Xylophone: A musical instrument you play by hitting different sized keys with a mallet.

Yo-Yo: A toy with two flat round sides with a string in the middle.

Zipper: A slider that moves along rows of teeth to fasten your jacket, jeans, or luggage. Named so for the sound it makes. ZIP!!!